W9-BKQ-999

T·H·E
SHAMAN
BULLDOG

A Love Story

RENALDO FISCHER

◆ WITH MICHELE St. GEORGE ◆

WARNER BOOKS

A Time Warner Company

Grateful acknowledgment is made for permission to reprint previously published material:

The Outermost House by Henry Beston, copyright 1928, 1949, © 1956 by Henry Beston. Copyright © 1977 by Elizabeth C. Beston. Reprinted by permission of Henry Holt and Co., Inc.

Copyright © 1996 by Dr. Renaldo Fischer
All rights reserved.

Warner Books, Inc., 1271 Avenue of the Americas, New York, NY 10020

A Time Warner Company

Printed in the United States of America
First Printing: July 1996
10 9 8 7 6 5 4 3 2 1

Library of Congress Cataloging-in-Publication Data

Fischer, Renaldo.
    The shaman bulldog : a love story / Renaldo Fischer, with Michele
St. George.
        p. cm.
    ISBN 0-446-52029-2
    1. Human-animal relationships—Fiction. 2. Dog owners—Fiction.
3. Bulldog—Fiction. 4. Dogs—Fiction. I. St. George, Michele.
II. Title.
PS3556.I764S48 1996
813'.54—dc20   95-52192
                                                                      CIP

Book design and composition by Giorgetta Bell McRee

To the magic of Faccia Bello, whose courage, life, and character inherently drove him to be all that he was in every moment, in the least and last of every splendid detail.

We need another and a wiser and perhaps a more mystical concept of animals. . . . In a world older and more complete than ours they move finished and complete, gifted with extensions of the senses we have lost or never attained, living by voices we shall never hear. They are not brethren, they are not underlings; they are other nations, caught with ourselves in the net of life and time, fellow prisoners of the splendor and travail of the earth.

—HENRY BESTON
The Outermost House

Dancing with Sister Death

*Dogs perceive the Otherworld. They bark
when spirits roam about and howl when
Death approaches.*

—GYPSY FOLK LEGEND

Faccia Bello howled in pain. It was more than
a howl. He screamed and shrieked from some
dark primordial level. When I tried to touch or
stroke him, he would twitch, shake, and scream
again. I have never been so close to such raw suffering.

My huge, awesome dog, a prime physical
example of his English bulldog breed, had lost ten
percent of his body weight in just three days. His

head hung so low that it touched the worn tile floor of the hospital's examining room.

The skin folds and the prominent muscles of his heavily bossed and sculptured forehead twitched in tremors so violent that his shedding coat dropped stiff white bristles on the floor tiles. I watched in terror, frozen and helpless as he cowered in shock and pain.

I tried to concentrate on finding a diagnosis, overcome by the dark notion that I would soon be required to put an end to his suffering. Fear blocked straight thinking. I knew little about animals, yet I knew much about what could go wrong with living human systems. In my radiology practice, the primary mission was to make a diagnosis. We use the latest tools, make pictures of problems, and find the pathology so that others could begin some form of known treatment. Yet never had I felt so directly responsible for an outcome, and a deep heartache spurred my confused thoughts.

Faccia Bello is Italian for "beautiful face." I had watched that beautiful countenance take on a moving car chin-first. It was the most recent of an unusual number of close calls in his short existence. Why were these life-threatening events so dramatic and frequent? Each new catastrophe pulled me from my normal stance as a distant, overworked, and stressed physician into a tenacious protector of another's life. Even my human patients did not invoke this level of emotional attachment. My professional armor always provided me with some distance and detachment from the painful mush of gathering love.

Was there purpose in all this suffering? Faccia Bello had hooked me deep into the mystery of life's suffering. Hope and despair took turns with me. How did this happen? Why couldn't I prevent it?

♦

It was Sunday about 7:00 P.M. and the Man called out, "Facci, it's time for bye-bye walk."

It was a familiar phrase to Faccia Bello, rising from the voices of the surface world. He had absorbed many of his family's ways of communicating and commanding him through body language, mood, or verbal tone. He put his own twist to his peculiar responses. The family rarely got exactly what they wanted, but always more than they expected. Faccia Bello enjoyed the art of surprise.

The walks were a chance to explore a neighborhood full of adventure and friendly people. Sometimes they would encounter that treacherous

German shepherd, or maybe he would get lucky and see the Cat. He loved to find the Cat and give chase until he was exhausted. Tonight as he heard the call, he heaved his sturdy frame off the cool tile floor, submitted to the leash, and followed the Man into the dark and starry night.

Faccia Bello hurried down the walk, and the Man had to run a little to keep up until they got to the grassy place by the park. This was his favorite place to take a dump, and as he did the Man cheered him on and said, "Good boy, Faccia Bello, good boy."

This lightened him considerably and he began to ramble about, sniffing and smelling the earth and flowers, savoring the aromas of other worlds. He inhaled the familiar scents of other cats and dogs who had marked their spots, as well as the pungent smell of a jackrabbit that came here to dine. He liked to bury his face in the soft and sometimes prickly bushes, breathing in deeply all the fragrances and feeling the energy emanating from so many different life forms. Some plants were so inviting that he would just start eating, leaves, twigs, and all.

"Don't eat the lantana or the ferns, Faccia," reminded the Man. "You'll get sick."

Faccia Bello was deep into these delights and the Man had to snap the leash two or three times to get him to quit. Lantana was an attractive delicacy and well worth the choking and retching that soon followed. He just couldn't resist some fatal charm of that plant.

Faccia Bello would pull so hard on the leash that he choked himself, and even while choking he would continue to pull until the one walking him danced around, and pulled in a competing direction against the bulldog's energy. His neck size was twenty-four inches, and with his weight, strength, and bulldog determination he couldn't be stopped.

Faccia Bello preferred to be walked in his immediate neighborhood, where he could escape the leash for a few moments to take his dump. After a few "Good boys," he would glance to see if the Man was watching and then he would break into his famous bulldog trot. That was when he became the most deceptive NFL flanker in the game. Maybe that had been his role in another life, when he led the league in receiving, yards per catch, and touchdowns. Faccia Bello would burst hard for fifteen yards, buttonhook, and look back over his shoulder, tossing his head as if to say "I'm unstoppable," then he would go deep, escape into the neighborhood, and the game to catch him was on.

Ignoring the pull, Faccia Bello charged ahead to the community fountain, a place of bubbling waters and shining reflections of light. The Man called, "Facci, you can't swim, so don't climb in the fountain."

Facci liked to stop here and pamper himself, wet his feet and take a drink. Faccia was particular about water. He wouldn't drink from a bowl; in fact, he would splash it around, step and even slobber in the water bowl, demonstrating his contempt for that whole idea of water delivery. He would drink only running water from a hose or from his special on-demand faucet that squirted water at him whenever he nudged it.

Across from the fountain was a busy street with many cars, roaring with energy and flashing light patterns in the water. Some of that energy grabbed Faccia Bello and said, "Go."

The Man lost hold of the leash and Faccia Bello ran into the moving lights. The nearest one was very large and fast, and as Faccia Bello turned to face the car, it crashed into him. Two charging bulls met, one large and one very small. Faccia Bello was tossed in the air with a sudden deep hurting and then the peace and darkness of unconsciousness.

◆

I carried the unconscious bulldog, bleeding from the mouth and nose, to the animal hospital. The vet on call said his examination revealed that

Faccia Bello had a severe concussion and some cuts and abrasions, including surface damage to the cornea of his left eye. Initially the outcome didn't look too bad, especially after the crushing hit he had absorbed. He was patched up and sent home the next day to recover. However, Faccia Bello quickly deteriorated and wouldn't eat or drink. Then he began his terrible howling.

We returned to the hospital and the small fluorescent-lit room, with a sink for hand washing and a countertop for the examination. As I squatted next to Faccia Bello on the floor, I recalled how much time I had spent down on my knees in the two years that he had been with me. Eye-to-eye contact gave us the opportunity to play, make up games, talk, massage him, and feed him snacks or medications. Mostly I just loved to study his wrinkled face, fascinated by this living work of art. Due to the extensive inbreeding of the bulldog line, Faccia Bello had many of the usual bony abnormalities in his face and snout. Huge shoulders supported a large round head. The squashed nose lost itself in ravines of short smooth fur, and a bulldog grin split the face ear to ear.

This peculiar facial structure produced a humanoid expression that was captivating. His large expressive eyes presented a variety of images to me, from grandfatherly wisdom to childlike impishness.

Here I was again on my knees in my culturally correct Italian renaissance finery, an Armani long-sleeve sport shirt, Zanella slacks, IGI & IGI multicolor sweater coat, and Bally shoes, a modern physician at his wits' end, reduced to fear, confusion, and emotional distress.

"Faccia Bello, what's wrong? I need to know what's wrong. I won't let you go and I can't let you continue to suffer."

The possibility of his death was now torturing me as much as his physical pain shredded him. Putting him to sleep was the outrageous option tugging at me. Where was the vet? Give my dog a shot of Demerol. This is very cruel and unjust.

Is this what being open and vulnerable to love and affection is about? My God, what a nightmare. No wonder in medicine we cultivate a professional attitude of care and leave aside these wild emotions and fears.

Faccia Bello screamed again just as his vet, Dr. Tomaso, slid open the door and came into the room.

"Facci, what's wrong, tell me what's wrong," repeated Tomaso sympathetically.

Tomaso and I were stumped for a diagnosis. We

knew some clue was missing. He said, "I've x-rayed his spine, chest, and lungs and they appear okay. His pelvis isn't fractured, and his limbs are okay. This is the way it sometimes goes with animals. They go to their end with unanswered questions. There is no veterinary coroner, so endings are left to life's mystery as we go on to other cases we can help."

"Why all this pain and screaming? What about pain medication? He was hit in the head. Is a neurologist available?"

"With his concussion, I don't want to depress his respiratory system with medication. No, there is no neurologist and we don't have a neurosurgeon, either. This is veterinary medicine. I had our internist look at him, and it all seems to be posttraumatic, maybe a subdural hematoma."

"Have you x-rayed his skull? Maybe there is a skull fracture."

"Renaldo, that's not something we would routinely do, but I'll try that and maybe we can learn something."

I left Faccia Bello in Tomaso's capable hands and returned to my office. Tomaso was a great blessing and had tended to my crisis-prone dog on many occasions. He is a repairer of broken animals and a gifted surgeon, humbly carrying his healing gift.

Later in the afternoon Tomaso's voiced boomed through my office phone. "Hello, Renaldo! Good news—we've found Faccia Bello's problem. His skull x-rays show the jaw is broken in two places. He must have taken the moving energy of the car's bumper straight on, all with his low-slung jaw. Wow, what a hit! There is an amazingly tough life force in this dog to have survived this."

"Have you fixed double fractures before? What outcome can I expect?"

"I think he'll be all right. I've seen this twice before, but in dogs much larger than Faccia Bello. Little ones hit in the head don't survive the initial 'hit by car' experience to come to surgery. I will operate and do wire fixations on both sides, but I want to wait a while until he has recovered further from his concussion. I don't want to put him to sleep and not be able to bring him back. The double fractures are tricky. We'll drive some holes and do some version of figure-eight wiring to make the jaw stable. I'll figure it out when I get in there."

"Okay, Tomaso, please do it soon, as soon as you can, or he may die from shock. My intuition's strong on this. Don't wait."

"Well, tomorrow is Thanksgiving Day. . . . Okay, I do it on Thanksgiving. What could be more appropriate? I will get my staff to come in about eight in the morning and we'll be finished before noon. Then we'll go home and eat the turkey. When I'm done, I'll give you a call."

I hung up the phone and stared out the window. The very real possibility of Faccia Bello's death began a reflection on the presence of death in my own life. In my training as a physician, I could arrive with patients at many crossroads along the diagnostic path, new risks requiring more decisions. They usually wanted it all laid out, no surprises and no time to pause on the threshold of life or death. It's taken for granted that the gods of medical science can give instant pain relief and then reverse or repair almost anything; we want to get back to our everyday lives without facing the unknown.

All diagnoses, no matter how minor, contain the possibility of the ending of life. There is the potential of death in a head cold, a cut finger, or a diabetic's infected toe. Death is a paradox, present wherever life is present. When I deny the reality of death, I fail to appreciate how amazing, uncertain, and dangerous life really is. Living in an illusion, I project and design my future as if I dominate time.

There are so many things in life we can control.

11

The Shaman Bulldog

We control our environment by turning down the thermostat; motion and speed by driving our car; sound by turning up the music. We have so much discretionary power in our hands. Yet our control and power is illusionary. We have little or no control over the moment of death.

I've never believed that death ends our story. I do not know what comes after, but I believe my soul to be an indestructible labyrinth, a fusing of the conscious and unconscious worlds. I would befriend the mystery of death as St. Francis did, when he personified it by calling it Sister Death. In the refusal to recognize Her powerful presence, I can easily ignore the greater mystery of life.

Some of my patients who have bravely faced Sister Death seem to discover a new, more seminal way to live. A curse ends up being a blessing as they begin to recognize the meaning and value of each moment and how choices and thoughts affect our lives. They sacrifice the shallow views of their lives and see the greater surprises possible.

It is a beautiful philosophy, yet this unexpected threat to Faccia Bello had flipped me into chaos and brought me to the brink of despair. How can I surrender to Sister Death when I don't want to let him go? I couldn't face the possibility of great personal loss. Some part of me is also a "bulldog," locked on to finding a solution that intuition told me was present. There may be another reality that could contain and magnify his soul, but I was determined not to release my grip on him yet.

The chance that Faccia Bello would depart created for me an acute awareness of how much this humble creature had enriched my own soul. So many comical and joyous moments that were hurried past rather than savored. Perhaps this is also the gift of Sister Death—the vision to fully appreciate the precious chance to enjoy each moment of soulful living.

2

Waiting on Memories

*And what of Nature itself, you say—that
callous and cruel engine, red in tooth and
fang? . . . if there are fears, know that
Nature has its unexpected and unappreciat-
ed mercies.*

—HENRY BESTON

Thanksgiving morning I sat alone in Phoenix,
waiting for Tomaso's call. As soon as I heard
the outcome, I planned to drive to beautiful Oak
Creek Canyon near Sedona to celebrate the day
with friends. Overnight the dark events of Faccia
Bello's accident were slowly being sweetened by

gratitude. We were both still alive, and intuitively I believed that we were locked in to a story that was not finished.

Faccia Bello had often accompanied us to Sedona and drew a crowd wherever he went. In his winter Scotch plaid sweater vest he was a splendid sight as he crunched through the snow, licking and eating as he went. Or he would sleep flat out on the wooden deck of the condo in his usual Sphinx-like posture. There he would accompany the faint sound of the bubbling creek with his own deep snoring, a symphony of many variable pitches, hitches, and whistles. Against that background and the majestic walls of Oak Creek Canyon, I had found it easy to become lost in a contemplative nostalgia. Faccia Bello was part of my active meditation process connecting me to the natural world. No matter what turmoil was brewing in daily life, the presence of Faccia Bello seduced my imagination into a dreamlike reverie of warm images and feelings.

The people of this nation had declared today a holiday in thanksgiving to the cosmic God who is generous and answers prayers, and I certainly was one who was very grateful. I felt some small internal rhythm shifting inside me, and I was helpless to stop its movement or direction.

Intuitively I felt that life's mystery placed Faccia Bello and me together for some purpose I couldn't yet fathom.

My whole life had been devoted to solving every problem through logic, the logos of the rational mind. Figuring it out, planning, preparing, educating myself, a process that managed life by applying the keen human intellect to ward off its uncertainties. It is a way of playing God with only limited power. However, there are always problems that will not come to any logical conclusion. Some mysteries can be solved only through the heart, and I was ill prepared for that style. How does a man live through the heart without becoming fainthearted or hardhearted, weak-hearted, or chicken-hearted?

Now, in a deepening attachment to this English bulldog, I was beginning to suspect what it must feel like to have a heart open and vulnerable, the logical mind stripped defenseless.

I certainly had no premonition of Faccia Bello's significance to me when he first entered my life. My wife was the one who wanted a dog. Not just any dog, but a runt-of-the-litter English bulldog. I was against this from the first conversation, because I knew the outcome. Our boys would grow tired of caretaking the dog, it would be a hassle to exercise him, and we would be pinned down and restricted with any travel plans. Despite my many protests, an $800 pup, the child of "Looking Good and Apple Dumpling McBull," arrived air freight from Denver one night in May. Suddenly there was a star boarder at the house and our lives took on a new order and a certain central focus.

His given name was Faccia Bello, "Handsome Face," but as time went on he was personified as Facciarelle, Facci, Bello Meo, or Mr. Bello. I later discovered that my Italian was faulty. Since the Italian word for face, *faccia,* is a feminine noun, I should have called him Faccia Bella. However, it still seemed wrong to my ears to pin feminine designation on such a virile beast.

What's in a name? Although we initially considered such titles as Faccia Brutto ("Ugly Face") and Duo Faccia ("Two Face"), I later realized how sadly inappropriate those designations would have been. Naming him "Beautiful Face" called forth his natural beauty and charm, which grew and evolved over the years until I could see him in no other light.

As a pup, Faccia Bello kept cool his first Phoenix summer by having a plastic wading pool to splash in and a little beach chair in which to bake dry while snoozing. I felt jealous arriving home from a long day and seeing him live the easy life.

He ruled as lord and master of the house in between six visits to the nearby animal emergency room before he was half a year old. The symptoms were always the same, difficulty breathing and choking. The emergency vets got to know him very well and said the same thing with each visit: "It's an aspiration pneumonia." He was treated with airway dilators and antibiotics. They had no idea why this happened so often. They said that was just the way bulldogs were.

The first time Faccia Bello nearly died created a permanent shift in our relationship. I was wakened by a shout from my afternoon nap. Faccia Bello was eating his supper and began choking. He was down, flat on the ground and not breathing. Furious and fearless, I blamed God for neglecting his creatures. There was no cause for this dog to die, suffocating from such an innocent activity as eating.

Faccia Bello's pupils were dilated and his tongue was purple blue. Clutched by the pain of loss, I lay on the ground next to him, my face in his. Through my curses and tears, I tried to kiss Faccia Bello good-bye. A kiss of death became a kiss of life as I unknowingly blew into his nose. Suddenly his chest expanded and he took a breath. In a short time he took many more breaths and turned a light shade of pink. Then he struggled to sit up, looking very groggy and beat up.

In that moment, the biblical declaration of Paul to Timothy sprang into my mind: "You are now my spiritual son." Faccia Bello had become in some imaginative way the son of my breath, my spirit, and my soul, indeed "my boy."

That unconscious act of artificial respiration, doggie style, produced a unique bonding between us. I didn't feel like a hero, but rather wondered at the instinct within me that knew what was needed to restore life. It allowed me to bring him back to life, using my own breath and life force. It was an "animal" instinct, that part of a creative life force that operates independently of logic and the rational mind. It was the spontaneous, creative spark that keeps the stories of our lives evolving in their own designs, unless thwarted by heavy conditioning and civilized manners.

The much maligned animal instincts may not create ultrasound machines or laser surgery, but as far as allowing them to live successfully on the earth and on the planet, their instinct is far superior to what we have.

Back in the emergency room, the diagnosis of his near death episode this time was a bee sting or allergic reaction. They were again guessing, and it was becoming embarrassingly obvious that no one seemed to really know what to do about Faccia Bello.

I asked around, and Dr. Tomaso was recommended as a bulldog expert. When I placed Faccia Bello into his care, I gained a friend and Faccia gained a lifelong ally and protector. Immediately Tomaso knew what was wrong. As he explained it, "A bulldog's palate can be too large for the throat. Usually when eating and trying to swallow, it gets caught on the epiglotteal valve which closes the airway, causing a respiratory arrest. If he chokes while eating, some of the food can enter the airways of his lungs and then he gets an aspiration pneumonia. This can occur over and over until the dog dies from lung scarring and pneumonia or airway obstruction."

A few weeks later Tomaso excised half an inch off Faccia Bello's soft palate, but not before he went into respiratory arrest again, this time while I was watching a Monday night Miami Dolphins–Chicago Bears football game. As Faccia Bello struggled for breath, I flattened him out on the kitchen floor, pushed on his diaphragm, thumped on his back, and blew in through his nose. I was becoming an experienced hand at canine recovery.

Faccia Bello recovered easily from his surgery, and his peculiar bulldog personality began to assert itself. He could make a great ritual out of moving chairs and other small pieces of furniture. He would push and pull up a dining room chair to sit with the family at the dinner table. It was a painstaking struggle for him to shove the chair into the right position and then slowly climb up, first the front feet inching in, then the balance of his head and chest moving forward over some imaginary pivot point. Then the slow command to the back legs, one at a time, as if this were a part of the nervous system he had to ponder in order to control. When he was up he sat down and faced the family with his little legs tucked under him. So our family of four became five when we were around the table and ready for grace.

He learned that I always exited through the kitchen door when I wasn't planning on taking him with me. So Faccia Bello began to move a kitchen chair into position in front of the door. When I would go to leave there would be Faccia Bello sitting on the chair, smiling his bulldog grin and blocking the way.

22

Life with Faccia Bello began quickly to bridge the gap between fact and imagination. Native American myths and legends always assigned humanlike actions to animals. Was I just discovering something they already knew? Faccia Bello was no longer just a pet, he was a myth in the making, with me as an interactive observer and his eventual scribe.

When I spoke to others about Faccia Bello's adventures, people listened in fascination. When these same people came to our home, the usual greeting was, "Hello, where's Faccia Bello?"

As I was beginning to explore the mystery of animal consciousness, Faccia Bello posed more questions than I knew how to answer.

One evening I was watching a New York Yankees ball game played against the Cleveland Indians. It was the ninth inning and the Yankees were losing 2–1. I had been a Yankee fan as a kid, and today Phil Rizzuto, a former Yankee great, was broadcasting the last innings. At this critical time in the game the call came from the kitchen, "Dinner is ready."

Unhappy with the timing, I got up and started into the kitchen just as Faccia Bello walked into the den and sat down. Usually he paid no mind to TV, but since we were trading places I said to him in jest, "Keep an eye out and tell me the final score."

Halfway through the main course I heard two very loud barks from the den. I got up to investigate and discovered that the Yankees had scored two runs in the last of the ninth inning and won the game. Faccia Bello barked not another word and walked away.

The phone rang and broke my reverie. It was Tomaso.

"It went fine. Facci is breathing on his own and waking up now. I was able to do a figure-eight fixation on the right side, and on the left I drilled some holes for a wire fixation with loop stabilization. It looks solid. His teeth are okay. We'll get him going tonight on water and gruel."

"Happy Thanksgiving, Tomaso! I'm very grateful. I wish you, your family, and all your animal clients the peace of many seasons."

Faccia Bello, my boy, was okay. I felt a surge of gratitude and joy. My prayers this Thanksgiving were poorly conceived but certainly more heart-felt, spoken in pain, emotion, and honesty. No longer the dogmatic prayers of my former high-flying spirituality, my words now spilled forth in a stuttering, stumbling emotion. I was more sure of the mysteries of life than its certainties.

After joining my friends in the ritual Thanksgiving meal, I stepped out into the crisp night air and saw a full yellow moon hung low in the sky, sharpening the nighttime shadows. I was connected to this world, the animals, plants, and people in it. Tonight it seemed a friendly world, woven together with the same elements of life, a natural magic and creative consciousness. I felt the cosmos to be beneficial and provident, showering us with a great grace. I had yielded to some deeper edges of my human struggle for heartfelt meaning and purpose.

3

Dreamtime Myth

The creatress known as "Our Grandmother" was accompanied by her small dog as she finished and perfected the world.
—SHAWNEE INDIAN MYTH

Under the deep spell of anesthesia, Faccia Bello found himself wandering through a strange, shadowy land. The medicine man and his powerful medicines had cast him into the Dreamtime, the land of Great Mystery.

A brilliant moon cast its light across a tree-studded landscape. A sky full of stars shed such a piercing light that Faccia Bello blinked several times to clear his vision. Lifting his massive bulldog head to the sky, he discovered to his deep delight that he could breathe easily now. The acrid smell of campfire smoke filled his nostrils, and he knew instinctively that there was someone else with him in this world, although they were some distance away. On his left a gurgling creek splashed its way across the landscape. The agonizing jaw and head pains were gone, and he drank deeply of the churning waters. How pleasant it would be to remain here.

It all seemed very real to Faccia Bello, yet he knew this was the space of deep dream, where shapes could shift and images could twist and converge. This was the Soul's realm, a dark underpinning to his everyday world. The urge to explore grabbed him and he trotted off in search of the campfire. He did not wish to be alone in this vast and unknown world.

He could hear them before he saw them. Low laughter and murmuring voices fell on his ears like music. Surely these would be friendly companions. As he neared the campfire, he saw them: a withered, weatherbeaten old crone and a young wolf staring into the flames. They looked up expectantly as Faccia Bello stepped hesitantly into their circle, unsure of his welcome. The Woman's lips parted in a toothless smile.

"Faccia Bello, Wolf and I have been expecting

your company. Quite a scare you gave us. You are not supposed to dance with cars."

Her warm chuckle encouraged Faccia Bello. He lay at her feet, glancing sideways at Wolf to make sure he was not offending. The Wolf's yellow eyes contemplated Faccia Bello without welcome or reproach. The crone stretched out a thin sun-browned hand and began stroking Faccia Bello's back.

"This Wolf is your most ancient ancestor, Faccia Bello. You have quite a marvelous history. From the Wolf I have created a vast nation of the Canine with many clan families. Back in the time of your clan's beginnings, I wove Man in a new image. Out of the forests and jungles came all the humans, struggling to live on the land with its vast resources and many gifts.

"Man struggled so hard to live, because he was not born with the fine instincts and magical powers of the animal nations. He could not smell the deer on the wind or hear the soft footfall of the rabbit, so he had to hunt long and hard for his food."

As Faccia Bello gazed adoringly into her face, he felt the gnarled fingers become part of a long and supple arm that felt feathery on his body. Eight shiny arms gradually encircled him, tenderly casting silken threads from their tips and encasing Faccia Bello in a warm cocoon. The withered body had become the supple and rounded form of a spider. Faccia Bello felt no fear at this sudden transformation. Things were always shifting shape here in the Dreamtime.

Her voice continued very high now, not like a human voice at all, and even higher than Faccia Bello could hear. He sensed her words rather than hearing them.

"I saw that Man needed a companion, an ally from the animal nations. And so I created the Canine with instincts uncommon to other beasts. Faithfulness, devotion, intuitive wisdom, instinct, and understanding surpassing those of Man himself.

"You have no power of words to cause disputes between you and Man. You are blind to his faults.

"These qualities I gave you from beyond time and from before the creation of the surface world. I have woven you into Man's world with threads of love and trust. Unlike his own kind, you will not know how to betray him."

Faccia Bello marveled at the creation story. His thoughts drifted pleasantly, relishing this time in the middle world, a world of no pain or fear. Many humans were afraid of this Dreamtime place, and now that Faccia Bello saw it again, he wondered why. Everything that was in the surface world was here

30

also, yet more powerful and alive. This is the pool bubbling beneath the surface of life, the place where poets hear their inspiration and artists recognize their images. Without this world, the other could not exist. It is a shadow mirror moving and dancing with the surface mysteries.

It was here his bulldog clan had first heard its purpose and been sent to the surface world with its mission. Here his clan remained in its figurative and imaginal forms, along with all the ancient animal nations, great winged creatures and massive beasts that moved into the sea, and the sea creatures that moved to the land.

As Faccia Bello opened his eyes, he found that he had been joined at the fire by new companions. A circle of elderly bulldogs sat around him, their wrinkled faces studying him intently.

A very ancient bulldog, glowing in a circle of light, spoke, and Faccia Bello recognized his grandfather.

"My young hero, you have made a great beginning of your mission in the surface world, but your work is far from finished. The upper world suffers from a lack of love. Man hides his feelings from his fellow humans.

"This Man has magical qualities that remain hidden in him. You will teach him to open to the mystery of his existence and the wonder of his soul. You will make him a lover, and you will be his companion and ally.

"Speak to him with your magical heart and honest eyes. Walk by his side, ward off his enemies, share his afflictions, love and comfort him. In return this Man will fulfill your simple needs of food, shelter, and affection and will provide you the special healing care you will need.

"You may be the only friend this Man has at certain times in his life, so guide him through the perils to the lands that have been promised him. And then this land too shall be your destiny and immortality."

Faccia Bello heard this summons, not so much in words, but through images, mutual instinct, and intuitive understanding, which is how things are communicated in the Dreamtime.

Faccia Bello was eager to help the Man, but he knew that the pain, suffering, and sickness that must be endured on the surface world is very underestimated. No wonder the humans lose heart.

His grandfather responded, "It takes much hardship. You and the Man will discover and realize your purposes together. You have been made prone to accidents and illness, so that he will be forced to focus on your great neediness with attention and involvement. His heart is good and he will respond to your chaos.

"You can stand pain, for your fierce bulldog clan was bred to bait bulls and endure the pain of conflict. Many perils still await you, but your ancestors and protectors in the middle world are supporting your life force of loving and courage. In your nighttime Dreamtime and in your snoring daydreams, Faccia Bello, we will communicate. When the Man has seen the beauty of your story, you'll finally return to us and be free to roam all worlds, as a wise and joyful soul."

Faccia Bello woke up in a cage at the animal hospital, head and jaw stinging with pain. He carefully worked his tongue around his dry mouth and hoped to fill his very empty stomach soon. Some running water would be nice.

4

A Contrary Teacher

*We patronize them for their incompleteness,
for their tragic fate of having taken form so
far below ourselves. And therein we err, and
greatly err. For the animal shall not be mea-
sured by man.*

—HENRY BESTON

Faccia Bello improved rapidly after his surgery. Once he could eat, he picked up weight and muscle and his chest expanded into the stature of a young maturing male bulldog. His white face was sharply outlined and demarcated about the snout, jowls, and lips as those regions lost the last remnants of pink fetal tissue and were now covered with a soft leatherly, richly black skin.

The dog show people said his head was a full "10" and he should be trained and shown in competition. I didn't have any energy or inclination to subject myself, let alone Mr. Bello, to the indignities of being primed up and driven throughout the state to be judged by others.

However, a little obedience training seemed in order. The natural world had given Faccia Bello a pure heart and no desire to follow orders. His independent stance could wear thin at times, as obedience was neither natural nor spontaneous to his nature. He was enrolled for a three-month course at the American Academy of Canine Behavior, which was extended to six months since he didn't seem to be getting it. Actually, he did appear occasionally to grasp the idea of submission, but only for a moment or two, and the concept didn't hold much interest for him.

It began with high hopes. The school's brochure boasted that its canine clients would become completely obedient to a number of important commands, which would even be followed off leash at the sound of the owner's voice.

The training began in the winter, at 7:00 A.M. each Saturday morning in the cold, dim light of dawn. The trainer worked intently at putting the bulldog through his paces. With each command or snap of the leash, Faccia Bello sought to translate the voice and awkwardly rearranged his body in what he suspected were the desired positions.

"Faccia Bello, sit!"
No reaction.
"Faccia Bello, no, sit!" (snap the leash)
"Faccia Bello, come!"
No reaction.
"Faccia Bello, no, come!" (snap the leash)

His strategy became quickly apparent. Ignore the first cue and move slowly on the second cue. When nothing worked the trainer simply shoved and bent him into the position required. To Faccia Bello, "Heel!" meant ignoring the first, second, and third commands, then being bodily dragged by the trainer along the cold cement of the sidewalk until he scrambled to his feet and trotted along. Each week we began again at the beginning. After six months of training, his bulldog stubbornness had stretched out his standard 6-foot leash to 6½ feet. The leash was compliant and adaptable. Faccia Bello's attention was elsewhere.

Finally I tired of the process and just watched the comedy between bulldog and trainer. By the fourth month I felt such sympathy for the trainer that I gave him an additional bonus. He had met the bulldog's mettle.

The trainer did prove valuable in several ways. He recommended the bulldog expert Dr. Tomaso, and also managed to teach Faccia Bello to ride in the back of my Jeep Wagoneer. The command for car rides was "Faccia Bello, bye-bye car!"

That was the only command that induced instantaneous response. He would bolt through the dog door and race to the garage. When the tailgate dropped, he threw his front paws on the gate and waited to be butt-lifted in. Faccia Bello turned out to be a great traveler, and he never dawdled or forgot the command. He posed regally in the rear of the Jeep, a bullgod deity who casually accepted the startled and approving glances of other drivers.

Faccia Bello liked noisy motorcycles. He would catch their engine roar as they overtook the Jeep. His eyes locked like radar onto the image and sound, his head swiveled to watch them pass, staying that way until they disappeared in the distance. What was routine to me was magical to him.

As I slowly became educated to Faccia Bello's spontaneous nature, I gradually dropped any concept of extended training. Just the simple and necessary stuff would be satisfactory.

"Faccia Bello, come!"

This command was always ignored, but he never failed to trot over instantly to me if I simply squatted down, getting on his level.

Once Faccia Bello had a consultation with a dog psychologist who helped us devise a system to keep our canine explorer out of the back carpeted bedrooms, where he liked to mark turf. I had been using a dog gate for years, and the wear and tear on my right hip became painful as I had to hurtle this gate several times a day. The orthopedist's advice was to stop the hurtling activity.

The psychologist came up with a white piece of clothesline marked with strips of black tape. This was placed on the floor in front of the hall doorway. Two inches above this was strung a piece of thread to serve as a trip wire, which was connected to a motion device. When Faccia Bello crossed the clothesline he tripped the wire, tipping the motion device, which began blasting a shrill burst of sound until it was shut down. At this point the dog was supposed to be startled and flee to safe ground, which Mr. Bello did like clockwork in his first try. After two or three more attempts to penetrate the sound barrier, he just stopped testing the system. He had been outfoxed by a Vietnam era–trained psychologist.

The device was now my problem. If I walked through the door, forgetting to step over the two-inch trip wire, then I set off the alarm, and it was I who was startled and chagrined. Faccia Bello just watched it all with little interest except to cast a critical eye at me when I sounded the alarm. Over time I was the one who was always falsely firing the alarm, and it was particularly dramatic when stumbling in the dark, late at night.

Faccia Bello was a "wood eater." Soft or hard wood yielded easily to his powerful jaws. All my end tables, coffee tables, and chair legs received the mark of the bulldog. Your turf was his turf. He lolled on a couch that he claimed for himself.

All methods to deter him proved futile. Faccia Bello didn't care for rawhide bones, hoof treats, plastic or rubber toys. It was wood he craved. The trainer gave me some foul-smelling liquid to be sprayed on furniture. He claimed, "All dogs just hate this. It's some kind of tobacco juice distillation." Faccia didn't mind it, nor did he mind the sour apple and sharp citrus scents that I tried next. Camphor worked for a short time, but as it evaporated the wood eater would strike again. Over the years I resigned myself that the house and its contents were not treasures and would have to be shared.

A two-gallon plastic milk carton was Faccia Bello's preferred toy. He grasped the handle in his mouth and raced away with it, or he chased it if it was kicked along the ground.

"Keep Away" was the only game he would play. He would fetch but not return. So I would fetch myself over to Faccia Bello and try to wrestle away the milk jug. This always resulted in hugs and rubs.

Thinking I could teach Faccia Bello to swim, one day I foolishly dropped him in the pool, perhaps reenacting my boyhood memory of being taught to swim in a similar fashion. Faccia Bello apparently had never heard of the "dog paddle." Without pedaling even a single stroke, he sank like leaded weight and stood on the bottom of the pool on all four feet, looking up toward the surface with little bubbles coming from his nose. Astonished, I jumped in, scooped him up, and put him on the pool deck. Faccia Bello shook the

41

water from his coat and simply walked away. Not a cough or a blink, just walked away dripping wet. I could almost see a cartoonlike bubble forming over his head:

"That was such a dumb idea, let's not even discuss it."

Then I hired a trainer to teach Faccia Bello to swim, but it was a furious struggle for him to stay afloat and he didn't like it. When he managed to clear the pool steps he ran into the backyard and hid. The trainer gave me a suggested teaching routine and with a wink of his eye left us to our own adventures.

From then on, Faccia Bello veered widely around the pool deck furniture, completely avoiding the edge of the pool so as not to tempt the water fates again.

He liked people and was always curious about every stranger and visitor. After the formal pat on the head he would withdraw a few feet away and sit, observing the interaction of humans. If anyone gave any sign of further interest, he would come over and present his backside for massage. He knew how to solicit and implore a massage.

Undoubtedly he had learned some lessons from the coyote, revered in the Native American myths as a trickster. He enjoyed posing near the large animal porcelain figures in my living room that served as end tables. Visitors would be startled when they saw a motionless goose-neck white swan, a baby elephant, and then an English bulldog that would suddenly shape shift and spring to life.

He was civilized to a point, but he remained true to his own bulldog nature. He was consistent in his obstinacy, never failing to dismiss the error of human ways when they did not seem to apply to him. Perhaps I began to recognize the degree of training I had undergone in society, the ways in which I had been overly socialized and civilized all my life by others. The rebellion and antisocial behavior of my youth, long since tame and unexpressed, had left me with a nagging hostility.

The thing I liked about Faccia Bello is that he would tolerate only so much. He showed his annoyance and anger by not coming when ordered or doing an inappropriate dump. It's a quality I've always liked about him. I like the bulldog in me.

Sigmund Freud once wrote in a letter that dogs give people an opportunity to give affection without ambivalence and a chance to admire a life free from the almost unbearable conflicts of civilization. Maybe this is why I grew closer to my uncivilized bulldog friend, who disdained the demands of the social order.

I wanted the freedom of living by instinct and intuition. Was Faccia Bello a message for me? Lost in the pain and mystery of a "midlife crisis," I really wanted to let go of expectations and turn a deaf ear to the critical, demanding voices in my life. I wanted to regain my soul's nature and freedom.

The expectations that I projected on Faccia Bello gradually gave way over the years to an easy acceptance of his nature. As I lost my nagging parent tone, Faccia Bello returned more unconditional loyalty and devotion than I had ever experienced in the human realm.

Faccia Bello entered through the heart rather than the rational mind. Gradually I found I had a heart that could be wide open to possibility and an imagination fully capable of engaging a visit from this other nation. He was a wonderful expression of the Deity, sent to companion me. I had met my match.

Certain people keep hoping for aliens to come, as if they would have easy answers to our difficulties as humans simply because they would be of a higher-order intelligence. We have other nations among us right now and we treat them like aliens, to be subjugated and exploited. I had come to the recognition that the animal nation and its emissary, Faccia Bello, were given in an imaginative and heartfelt way to engage the alien aspects within my own soul.

5

Walking and Winged Reflection

The world today is sick to its thin blood for lack of elemental things, for fire before the hands, for water welling from the earth, for air, for the dear earth itself underfoot.
—HENRY BESTON

O ak Creek Canyon in Sedona was a favored hiking spot for Faccia Bello and me. Majestic red rock cliffs and a shady forest land were a welcome respite from the desert heat of Phoenix. Early one morning Faccia Bello and I were walking along the west fork of Oak Creek through the canyon's woodlands. The air was clean and cold and carried our breath in small clouds. We walked on a carpet of fallen maple leaves, soft and springy, a spectacular foundation of crackling sound and color.

Faccia Bello was sniffing and investigating every sight and movement on the woodland floor as well as the delicate white flowers that hung on low branches. Mossy rocks offered numerous spots to signal his turf, and that morning he marked and claimed some very valuable real estate as his own. One very large, multicolored leaf caught his attention, and he carried it with us as a treasure. Then I found a splendid rusty red leaf, so we both carried huge fan-size leaves. It was a spontaneous celebration of beauty and freedom as we strolled along, feeling a crackling energy and vitality that we rarely felt in the city.

In this lush natural setting, I remembered stories I had heard of that great lover of nature St. Francis, who had magical connections to the forests, woodlands, animals, and winged creatures, especially his friends the birds. His mystery and legend spoke of the out-of-season blooming of almond trees and flowers, birds who came to sit on his shoulders and fingers, and an intimacy with the elemental energies that he called Brother Sun, Sister Moon, Brother Wind and Fire, Sister Water, and Sister Death. Most wondrous of legends was his season living with Brother Wolf.

Such a simple and profound quality of life seemed hopelessly remote to me, a modern man with a modern medical practice that relied on the wonders of science and machines to work its miracles. Were there really such magical connections in creation as Francis saw? The mystery seemed so close that day in Sedona, almost as if I were breathing the same air as Francis.

Francis was a radical, and the people in his town called him mad. He had sacrificed life in a wealthy family and all his fantasies about fame and success in order to live on God's charity, dependent on nature and the animals for his companions. In turn he was honored by creation itself.

What was called the "Franciscan doctrine of animal soul" was quickly stamped out by the Church, providing an excuse for their cruel exploitation as mere commodities rather than the mysterious manifestations of creation that Francis knew them to be.

My soulful bulldog, Faccia Bello, had been honored by the spirit of this saint. On the October Feast of St. Francis, the Franciscan priests sprinkle holy water in an elaborate ritual called the

"Blessing of the Animals." Faccia Bello joined a chorus of canine, feline, and avian voices that perhaps talked to the spirit of Francis that day and saw his laughing response. I wondered what had prompted me to bring Faccia Bello to that particular ceremony, for it was certainly outside the realm of my normal spiritual practices and beliefs at the time.

Faccia Bello was becoming a gateway to a natural world that my soul craved. When I was with him, my unconscious constantly prodded me to stop, look, and listen, to see if I could see the same magic that Francis saw.

Now in some imaginal and intuitive sense I could understand the way of Francis, personifying and calling all things sacred, calling us to a new intimacy with each other and with creation itself. I had considered only the god in man and studied human beings for inspiration. Francis searched the nonverbal created nations and found God.

Faccia Bello was becoming a teacher, a guide and education for my soul in ways that I could not yet begin to understand. Native peoples cherished their connection to the "power animals" given to guide them by the Great Spirit. Was that happening in my parallel world, a rational, two-footed white skin world?

WALKING AND WINGED REFLECTION

♦

Pausing for a rest in their walk, Faccia Bello dropped the many-colored leaf and covered it with his paw, thwarting the Wind that might try to grab such a marvelous treasure. A flock of startled sparrows took flight from a nearby tree, and Faccia Bello looked longingly up at them. Birds are so quick and light, effortlessly reaching for the sky. "Bye-bye car" was Faccia Bello's only chance to fly, racing across the earth, though not very high.

Do birds breathe easier so far from the earth? A bulldog's squashed-up nose seemed constantly short of air. At least he didn't have to look very far for food. A large bowl was always reliably waiting for him at the end of the day, while the birds seemed to be constantly scrabbling for a few morsels.

One fine day Faccia Bello had seen the birds in a winged victory over the Cat. Eight mockingbirds in a furious, squawking cluster were flying high and then rapidly dive bombing something hidden by the hedge. As Faccia Bello curiously studied the drama, a black Cat suddenly burst out of the hedge, loping low and trying to duck his head from the furious onslaught of the birds. Three or four mockingbirds landed on his head at once, sending little tufts of black fur flying.

The Cat raced up a tree and they pursued him there. Finally he escaped into the very densest part of the hedge, where they couldn't peck him. Even then the birds didn't give up as they flew and swooped and shrieked in unison. Driven by the noise, the Cat tore out of the bushes as fast as he could, and the birds finally let him escape.

The world seemed to be a constantly unfolding drama. On their desert patio at home, Faccia Bello could watch spiders weaving delicate feathery webs one painstaking thread at a time, while bug wars raged between scurrying ants and fat black beetles. Plump quails with their jaunty black plumes arrived often, snatching the pellets of corn and sunflower seed that the Man left for them. Jeweled humming-birds slipped their pointed beaks into fleshy flowers and flew wildly up, down, sideways, and backward in an acrobatic dance. High overhead, the red-tailed hawk soared in lazy circles, always on the lookout for rabbits and mice. At night, Faccia Bello liked to snooze under a full moon and hear the coyotes sing.

◆

I was enjoying our stroll here in the cool mountains of Sedona, but Faccia Bello had gradually taught me to appreciate the desert as well. I was not happy twenty years ago when I moved to Phoenix. I would not be able to live along the ocean or in a forest or by a running creek. I was giving up a rhythm that I had acquired on the East Coast.

The desert was easy to dislike. Six months of staggering heat and summer temperatures well over one hundred degrees. Sharp needled cactus that punctured you with their daggers if you got too close. A vast dry world that sucked the moisture right out of your skin.

Now I've begun to understand that those first early desert years were a perfect mirror for my inner world. Empty spaces without any sense of moisture, little spontaneous life, hidden and unfamiliar territory. No buildings, no hustle and bustle to cover the emptiness. Too much distance and territory unclaimed and untamed by other men, and without a foothold I spiraled downward without wetness, vision, or imagination. The desert was a metaphor for my soul.

I had been seduced into moving west with scenes of a new life in California by the Pacific Ocean. I was waylaid by forces greater than myself, four hundred miles short of my goal in this arid desert. This was to be my last stand against the personal demons that were engulfing my soul.

The Shaman Bulldog

A lifetime of being negative, moody, and brooding had left me in the darkness of hopeless chemical addiction. No treatment or therapy had ever worked through my denial. Love had not penetrated the veil of isolation and self-condemnation. No wonder my initial experience in the desert was so deceptively colored. Sobriety began eighteen years ago and has remained solid. Yet still I resisted this desert that had mirrored the empty shell of my inner life.

Faccia Bello did not express a similar aversion toward the desert. Quite the contrary, in the cooler autumn, winter, and spring seasons, he would pull me off the path surrounding our patio home and drag me into the desert expanse. He took me where I didn't choose to go, and so began a series of desert journeys with Faccia Bello that have remained a great source of nostalgia and pleasure.

Faccia Bello was a house dog with soft feet. The desert nettles and burrs were tough on his pads, yet he would explore until he couldn't move, limping, crawling, and furiously licking the source of his pain. Many times I had to carry him home like a prince on a pillow, struggling under his seventy-pound bulk. Once he recovered, his enthusiasm returned undiminished and he would again drag me with him into the desert.

Eventually I arrived at a plan. There was a large, fairly flat region nearby that seemed safe, with less growth, fewer sharp rocks, and no prickly cactus. I brought a long nylon climbing rope, added it to his leash, and secured him to a bush or large rock.

Now he could explore within eyesight, and I was free to climb a small hill nearby and relax on a natural rock seat. From here I could survey a wide panorama of the desert, surrounding mountains, and the city spread out below. My vantage point was below a large twenty-foot Saguaro cactus. From our home it had appeared to be a single trunk, but now seated by it with a different perspective, I could see it actually was two huge trunks and a single root.

As I smoked my pipe the details and images of my little desert kingdom revealed themselves to me. Often Faccia Bello would turn and face uphill, barking furiously to signal me to come down or why couldn't he come up? Then he would fit his body into the ground or stake out space under a bush and take a nap. The breeze would bring the contentment of his snoring uphill to me, informing me that all was well in our world.

Slowly peace arrived in my solitude, and I began to cultivate an appreciation of the patterns of beauty in the small rugged plant life that expressed such a vigor to survive in this harsh environment. Sometimes we would visit before sunrise or after dark when a full moon would illuminate the landscape.

We both enjoyed watching the large jackrabbits that live on the hill. It was a game to see if we could spot one hiding in the bush with its long translucent ears lit by the sunlight, giving away its position. With my preliminary acceptance of the desert next door, we made some field trips to spots where there were marked trails so Faccia Bello could walk along as well.

One typical drive was to the White Tanks mountains an hour west of Phoenix. Near Waterfall Canyon Drive, I put Faccia Bello on a leash, grabbed my backpack and water bottle, and we started to walk.

There was a crisp breeze the entire way and windsongs in the canyon. In the early light small wrens pecked for seeds throughout the underbrush and ignored us.

I inspected several barrel cactus closely. They bore the heavy, sharp, impenetrable armor that kept me cautious in my approach, yet they were quite vulnerable to the birds that dined on the succulent blossoms and fruit. These winged crea-

tures in turn carried the seeds of new life throughout the territory.

Questions bounced through my mind. Why
did the barrel cactus need so much protection?
Who was their enemy in past generations? Who
hurt them so that now they live such hidden pro-
tected lives? It was as if I could feel the breath of
every living thing around us. All in creation was
connected, a single thread of consciousness unit-
ing us.

What had caused me to live hidden for so long?
Which wound—a word, parent, shame, or the
wind? So I waited helplessly, not whole and not
healed. I fell away from human life, hiding behind
barbed needles like the cactus. I had grown silent,
only breathing and maybe waiting for the forces of
transformation.

My leader was a little distance ahead, as I had
dropped his leash. He led me to some massive
boulders, some larger than houses. I wondered
what god came through here and dropped these
along the trail. The guide book said "granite out-
croppings." I thought my version just as valid,
and I'm sure ancient men thought the same.

I lifted Faccia Bello onto the craggy rock.
Standing on these boulders, I felt the solidity of
the earth, a tangible and impermeable mass. The

pull of gravity seemed almost a physical presence, much more so than when walking on the trail. So it was here we stopped for a while and had breakfast.

Farther up the trail we discovered rock petroglyphs. Some I recognized as symbols of the Saguaro cactus, one looked like a six-legged dog, and others were more universal signs. Why did they want to mark this spot? *We were here, we are strangers in a strange world and we were here.* All I could reply was that I see your sign, your medicine, your art.

The ancient man had left his art, his ritual, his petroglyphs. The modern man had shot hundreds of holes in the huge water tank that was placed here to water range cattle. Water so precious for life in the desert had its container destroyed. Modern man with his weapons has evolved into a very primitive form. Despite all his great technology, he no longer knows how to live on the earth.

For years I tried to find the divine in nature. Formulas rarely worked. Some of nature's best spots seemed overcrowded to me. Yet here in this deserted, remote canyon I experienced more peaks and insights into the sacredness of the natural world than I had in my entire lifetime.

This modern man had begun to discover new

territory. Now he was interactive, reading images and processing them through imagination. With Faccia Bello and the natural world as teachers, I had found a new mirror in the arid wasteland.

The vast desert had given me a looking-glass entry into my own inner landscape, a lonely and parched wilderness. My soul had made remarkable adaptations to the harshness, surviving as did the desert creatures—a small cactus wren nesting in thorns, a horned lizard hiding under a boulder, a tiny hedgehog cactus facing the blazing sun—all waiting to rejoice in the springtime rains that will revive us. The same vital life force that drives the desert to survive and adapt to these unfriendly conditions also drives my soul. I am the desert.

Whether crunching through deep leaves in Sedona or wandering the untamed desert, Faccia Bello was leading me into a nonverbal, nonintellectual world. These sacred places invite knowledge of ourselves when we honor their rhythm and dance. The natural world teaches us its eternal wisdom quietly. In the silence of our solitude, my bulldog and I breathed the same sweet, fresh air as the Sedona pine trees and rested gently to the heartbeat of a great desert mountain.

6

Dream Walkers

*Whenever a person loves a dog, he derives
great power from it.*

—SENECA SAYING

A marked change in my relationship with
Faccia Bello began to occur when he was
about four years old. In a remarkable dream I
began to recognize him as an individual soul
whose drama and destiny was running parallel to
mine.

Dreams keep me from living my life in the con-
straints of the literal world, with its ego-driven
justifications hidden in the personality masks. I

61

used to take this surface labyrinth much too seriously. I lived a self-important story that focused only on outcome and winning. Later I discovered that this surface existence was far more illusory than my dream images from psyche's world.

The gods of rationality and psychology are often in conflict when trying to explain the rich imaginative images of the dream state. Dreams are works of art and drama. Their soulful imaginal language becomes a powerful ally and teacher, connecting bridges to other worlds and realms of the unconscious.

Certain dreams seem deeper in their capacity to consciously educate me about what lies hidden. When I can consciously retain these interior images, my intuition in the surface realm seems expanded, senses become heightened, and perceptions beyond the rational mind hold sway. I can sense something is crouching in each ordinary moment, waiting to manifest.

These dreams become peak mystical experiences, a shadow-cutting knife revealing other dimensions of being that lurk below the surface of life to disclose the mythic and timeless nature of my soul's journey. I no longer believe dreams to be malleable by the rational psychology of "dream analysis." They are a separate world of their own, great creative works to be contemplated without jumping to active analysis or reconstruction. They are "the way it is" in the dark light of the soul.

Faccia Bello was my companion in one such dream state as I slipped into that unconscious other world one starless night.

As I leave the adult education class that I'm attending at a local university, I find the outside world has changed into a strange, unfamiliar wasteland. I don't know where I am. This isn't the same neighborhood, and I can't get my bearings. I'm in a futuristic fire-bombed urban city, a *Road Warrior* set with everything broken down to basic elements. I don't recognize any streets and I can't find my car, so I start walking, a stranger wandering in a strange land.

The night sky is black, with only yellow glowing streetlights for illumination. I walk along without any sense of direction until I am joined by an old woman whom I think I know, and we begin to walk together. In the background I occasionally hear a barking dog. I tell her my story, how everything is changed, different, and I don't know where I am or why I am here. I ask her, "Do you know where I can find my car? I don't see any cars anywhere. This is such a different world."

The Shaman Bulldog

She smiles without reply to my question. She points out that I'm not alone. My English bulldog, Faccia Bello, is walking here unnoticed at my side. We arrive in a warehouse district, and the woman pauses at the first doorway, says this is her place, and offers to take Faccia Bello inside while I continue to look for my car. Inside the house, other dogs are barking.

I agree to her suggestion and continue my search. Soon I come to a house with lights burning in large curtainless windows. Through the window I can see the figure of my son with some of his friends. He greets me at the front door and is surprised and happy to see me. I tell him I'm lost and I've lost my car. He offers to help and goes looking with me to find the car and to pick up Faccia Bello.

We can't find the car but end up back at the woman's warehouse, where we hear many barking dogs inside. I open the door and we find ourselves in a large living room. Neither Faccia Bello nor the old woman is present. The room is packed with energized barking and dancing dogs. Their heads appear normal, but their bodies are completely transformed into clear, translucent tropical fish bodies. Their flesh is a splendid transparent material, iridescent, colorful, marked and decorated with brilliant graphic designs and shapes.

The dogs dance around the room easily, jumping and barking joyfully. I am shocked and think someone has done radical experimental surgery, switching heads and using a new body material. Faccia Bello isn't here, and I am deathly afraid that I will soon see just his disconnected head.

I badly want my dog back. The old woman has made him disappear.

I woke up still in the grip of the dream. I couldn't shake the feeling of abandonment and loss. I raced into the living room and there was Faccia Bello sleeping on the couch. The dream still held sway over the surface reality. I couldn't believe that I hadn't lost him. I touched him, spoke to him and woke him up. He was still here, yet I clearly saw him in the dream world as well. The power of these dream images lingered for days.

In the dream my soul had journeyed to another dimension of psychic reality in which I had glimpsed a vast and infinitely rich realm of imagination.

Why such dramatic detail and the wrenching emotions of losing Faccia Bello? The old woman seemed to know him, and she could make him follow her and disappear. She had the power of transformation, the ability to make dogs into the new creation I had witnessed. When Faccia Bello's soul goes home, will he be a dancing dogfish?

The dream images carried me far beyond the rational, prevalent Western world view of animals. I did not then have any significant understanding of native peoples' views or consciousness, yet the dream revealed to a modern Western man a striking and timeless image of the canine nation. These dogs were deities in my dream world, shape shifters who danced and rejoiced at their sudden transformation.

As Faccia Bello had accompanied me in the dream world, I knew his soul was mysteriously connected to me in this surface world as well. We are much more than a moody owner and an obstinate pet. Our purpose together is to deepen soul.

The traditional religious view is that we may increase soul by ascending ever higher into the rarefied realms of purified and light-driven spirit. In the Renaissance they saw the maturation of soul as a descent, a constant growth down into the unknown realms of imagination, beauty, and wonder. Deepening soul pulls us far below the surface of life, into the ever-expanding mystery of the rich subterranean pools of the unconscious.

In these fertile depths of what Jung called the collective unconscious, I was making early discoveries, one of which is that there are many other nations in league with the human. I certainly knew I wasn't the center of the world. Losing that arrogant security, I began a quest to reconnect with the mystery of being in the world.

The native peoples have always understood the unity and connections between all creation. They consider having just one significant, sacred dream enough to envision their entire lifetime.

In the years since having this dream, I have gradually come to see Faccia Bello in a shamanic sense. Being a physician, I'm in the modern medicine man clan, so it is a natural notion. Shamans may be healers, magicians, or warriors, and they have existed in every culture since the beginning of time. Whether European, African, South American, Celtic, Asian, or native North American, we all have the ancestral memories of an ancient shaman inside us.

Shamans believed that everything has a life force, a soul. They acquired their powers from the natural world and so understood the weblike connections between ourselves and all of creation.

The Shaman Bulldog

Shamans talked with animals, plants, and rocks, with the spirits of Wind and Fire.

Some modern-day shamans attempt to alter their states of consciousness, as did the ancients, by ritual drumming, ecstatic dance, or even hallucinogenic drugs. Others spontaneously discover the shamanic states of consciousness, as I did, through the appearance of a "power animal."

The shaman has to have a guardian spirit in order to do his work, so a power animal presents itself to him, often in a dream, as a link to the massive power and energies of the natural worlds.

Many shamans are given eagles, bears, hawks, or mountain lions as their power animal. Apparently the universe decided I would need a bulldog.

A Tale of Two Bachelors

Sirius, the Dog Star, can be seen following his master Orion through the winter night sky. The gods banished the pair from earth, yet recognized their need for companionship even in exile.

—GREEK MYTH

Faccia Bello remained as my companion and guardian spirit when my well-organized, carefully planned life was ripped apart.

Divorce came as a particularly unwelcome surprise because my wife and I believed our marriage to be a "done deal"—it was forever. We were both dedicated to our unfolding spiritual journey and supported each other in our need to grow. Surely this marriage was destiny, so I adopted her two young boys, we furnished a house and built our little nest. Faccia Bello was very much a part of our lives. We enjoyed discussing him when I came home from work every night. "What did our boy do today?" He was more unpredictable than our sons.

Years later, when the boys grew up and left home, a mysterious estrangement wedged itself between my wife and me. Suddenly the things we had always liked about each other slipped into the background. We were both painfully aware that flawed, unrecognized parts of ourselves were beginning to emerge with a frightening energy of their own. It is one of life's mysteries—how does the "ideal couple" lose the love and certainty? Whatever force brought us together now seemed to be rending our bond and thrusting us out on our separate paths to discovery.

Chaos finally had its way, and my wife moved out of the house.

During the divorce process, one question repeated itself. When did the love between us cease? Had I ever permitted myself a complete, open-hearted surrender to love? It was obvious I had loved on a conditional level, and now I faced the guilt and self-accusations of one who has failed to meet another's needs, of one who has caused pain.

I was moody, and although I could sometimes be open and friendly with people in general, others often perceived me as hostile. I wanted a true, deep, intimate relationship, yet my heart remained hidden and well defended. I needed to be in control and simply didn't trust the process of "letting go." I interrogated myself, "Do I have any capacity to love unconditionally? Does anyone?"

The first year was very difficult. I was truly alone for the first time in many years. All our friends had been couples, and they no longer seemed comfortable with a single person. The separation process, financial and legal battles, ruled the days and loneliness the nights. I felt lonely, vulnerable, defensive, unsure of how to go forward with no way to go back. The future was no longer in my hands. It was a mystery beyond my control.

In the aftermath of questions and guilt, I needed some lightheartedness and joy. Faccia Bello filled the void, and my energy became spontaneously available to him. He didn't talk back, denigrate, or lay out expectations, he just loved

71

me as I was. I didn't have any need to control or run his life. We were on a level playing field.

Faccia Bello and I were alone to work out our destinies. He roamed freely throughout our home, entering and exiting a large doggie door at will, drinking from an autofaucet whenever he wanted, and sleeping anywhere he chose, usually on the red Mexican tile floor or his own couch in the living room. It was actually a love seat, just big enough for him to get a full stretch. Such a big lug, such a sweet goof. It was always a wonderful feeling to treat him swell, lavishly and richly.

Often he chose to sleep on the porch chaise longue, which overlooked a desert hill to the east, offering spectacular, cloud-filtered sunrises, with the large Saguaro cactus watching our activity. Faccia Bello preferred that spot when the nights were cool and starry. When the moon visited, her light never kept him awake. It was as if he knew her for centuries and now sang her his loud, sonorous song of Dreamtime.

When he decided to sleep or nap in the daytime, it was usually on the front patio, where he got to watch the rabbits eating lawn grass and the ongoing theater of the many birds. When I was first divorced I wanted to come to some new understanding with Faccia Bello about his care, to work things out so we both would not just survive, but feel good about life again. About that time a man saw us together at an espresso coffeehouse. He admired Faccia Bello and gave me his phone number, saying, "If you ever have to give him up, I will gladly take him and give him a good home." I put his number in my wallet.

Periodically it crossed my mind that life would be better for the both of us if I gave him away to someone with fresh energy and interest. Surely it would be much easier for me, adjusting to single life. I would have only myself to care for, coming and going when I wanted, no problems leaving town and no worries about kennels. The more I pursued this line of thinking, the more clearly I began to recognize my own selfish interests. It was essential that I be faithful and see through to the end at least one long-term relationship.

My heart spoke to me straight. We were meant to stick it out together, no quitting, no running, no convenient arrangements. With his many accidents and ill health, Faccia Bello needed my resources to keep him going.

Perhaps now I could admit that my developing compassion for Faccia Bello was the closest to an unconditional love I could claim. This bulldog I could love through his misfortunes, illness, and stubbornness, through the inconvenience of caring for him now that I was alone. What first started as compassion became a deeper and richer form of love. As long as I could continue to keep this love channel open, perhaps I wouldn't sink completely into self-centeredness and darkness.

So I refused to consider giving him up. As I supported him in his misfortunes, so he was to become my guardian spirit, my "power animal" that would teach me more about living and loving than I had ever been able to learn alone.

Faccia Bello missed the feminine nurturing of his daytime companion. My wife used to feed him, brush him, and take him for rides. I was trying to learn to be independent and take care of myself, shopping, and our home. My work made the days easy, but I came home tired every night with seemingly endless new duties to complete. I had never been happy in Phoenix, especially in the scorching summers, but now I didn't have the energy spark to move away, so Faccia Bello and I lived on here, making a home the best we could.

It became my responsibility to give Faccia Bello the nurturing, conversation, brushing, and care he needed, and he wouldn't be ignored. My office practice was full time during the weekdays, and I played homemaker in the evening and on weekends. Dreary, boring days stretched out endlessly, and I felt it would never change.

I was also shocked back into the singles world. When I had left twenty years before, I knew what was happening and even could make it happen. Now my attitudes were politically incorrect. Gender wars had reached a new level, with casualties on every side. If the anger between the wounded men and women didn't put loving relationships and intimacy on the back burner, then AIDS was taking romantic love, passion, and Eros to new cautious lows. Heart was a forgotten ingredient. What a bad time to come out.

The "meet your match" fad was in place, and singles ads attempted to match up the combatants by common interests, hobbies, activities, and values. If a relationship could be broken down into its component elements and if you managed to assemble enough of the right parts, everything was supposed to fall into place. Or you could just settle for some of the parts. Hopefully you would find a reasonable facsimile of a companion. Love, spontaneous attraction, and risk taking were out of the question, and soulmates were on the endangered species list.

My heart was not in that process, so I abandoned it early. My surrender was to the cosmos, and my prayer was to be open to surprise and the possibility of what luck would bring my way for soul's sake. With no immediate help coming from a new love interest, I kept busy with Faccia Bello, and gradually a peace and serenity came to our way of life.

Ever since his collision with a car he had an intermittent infection in his left eye. Now his right eye was involved, and neither one would clear with antibiotic ointment. As the problem worsened I took him to see Tomaso.

Tomaso said, "Faccia Bello needs plastic surgery."

"You are surely kidding me," I replied.

"No, I've had to do this on other clients. Antibiotics won't work. His forehead skin folds are so massive that his eyelashes have nowhere to go but up against the lenses of his eye. This causes chronic pain and mechanical irritation, which antibiotics cannot cure. You have to get to the source of the mechanical irritation."

So Faccia Bello had a radical face lift. When he returned home, his large beautiful head seemed half its size, with a great scar and stitches extending from ear to ear across the top of his forehead and below the eyes as well. What a pitiful sight.

His massive show dog look was replaced by a woeful countenance.

Faccia Bello had always seemed to be a great soul trapped in a bulky and awkward body. His movements were slow, and shifting positions took concentration. He would run only short distances as part of a game, and he had no interest in leash walking. Wandering and meandering through the natural world were what appealed to him.

A few days after surgery he was back in high spirits. The radical face lift cured the right eye and partially helped the left side, which nevertheless still continued to require twice daily cleaning and antibiotics as maintenance.

As he aged he developed a chronic sinus infection, with the left nasal passage dripping intermittently. This put him on a variety of antibiotics, both as external salves and in pill form. These little problems required daily attention, and he sat peacefully most of the time as we cleaned and cared for each problem.

Tomaso said, "I'm amazed how gentle and patient he is, even when poked, prodded, and stuck for blood work." The medical chart at the hospital had grown two inches thick over the years.

We went about making the living process more

manageable by enlisting the services of professionals. Our housekeeper was a young woman named Circe who straightened up the home on Wednesdays. Faccia Bello abhorred the vacuum cleaner, whether it was live, noisy and busy, or just sitting in plain view. The vacuum was his red flag, a bulldog's time to play "Attack the Beast," after which Circe would console and pet him. He certainly knew how to get people to touch him.

Every Friday Delilah would come by in her mobile grooming van and Faccia Bello would dash out for his bath and his body rub. She said she never had a client who would run to the bath; usually they just ran and hid. Faccia Bello's affirmative behavior allowed him to spend more than an hour each week closed up in the van with her and the fragrant soaps she used. She really appreciated his lovable nature, and he found the feminine energy he needed.

I scheduled a massage for myself at home every Tuesday night, and when the massage was finished, Calypso would give Faccia Bello his own additional time of professional rubbing. So the two bachelors got along in rather high style.

Some mornings I would scramble two eggs and add them to the dry dog food. He ate that with relish and gusto. In the evening I fed him a senior citizen–type dry dog food, which he finally refused to eat, strongly barking his dislike. I had bought forty pounds of it, so I tried tricking him by adding moist dog food consisting of rice and lamb. He liked that very much and was quite pleased for a while, and then he put up a fuss about that. Other dog owners would tell me not to let him be boss. It's very difficult to apply regular training rules to a bulldog, and I hadn't the time or fortitude, so I just learned to do it his way.

He shed his short-haired coat year round, so each morning and almost every night we would sit in the garage with the door opened to the street. I sat on a low lawn chair and he next to me. With one hand I would brush his coat and with the other smoke my pipe, read the paper or some poetry, and sip hot coffee. We passed many peaceful and contented hours.

He would watch the street for the cat and after a time fall asleep and begin to snore. In many ways it was quite ordinary, yet in that continued process of caring and loving my heart was opening fully to this fellow creature, willing to be vulnerable to the knowledge that I wouldn't have him forever as company. Long months and short years passed by.

One day I noticed his coat was very dry with

some areas of redness and loss. I called for an appointment and took him to Tomaso. He observed that Faccia Bello was living on the wire, already having outlasted by far the normal life span of his bulldog breed in a desert climate.

I came home with the new notion that I was living with a wise animal, an elder who in his own clan would be very distinguished and honored. Sometimes I had to admit I still regarded him as a burden or chore, inconvenient to my schedule and interfering with my ability to care for myself.

Tomaso's words hit deeply, and I suddenly began to see him in a unique way. Old images such as master or pet owner were never very strong. A larger point of view was that he was a bulldog elder and was outliving his clan's expected lifetime, a unique, sovereign expression of God's creation. There was a certain wisdom and purpose for us both through our aging relationship. I had done well in caring for him, and his personality and contrary nature were a perfect mirror of my own nature, which indeed someone might find lovable one day.

Bonded to me long ago when my spirit breathed life into him, Faccia Bello gave me unconditional love and loyalty, both never more evident than in the past year as we "bachelors" made our way together. His presence was always a comfort against the chill of loneliness and the nights of despair.

I remembered one of my favorite stories of Ulysses and his dog, Argos. After almost twenty years of life's adventure, Ulysses returns home a changed man. Although he had long anticipated his reunion with friends and family, no one recognizes him because he looks like a beggar. Only his devoted dog, who had been turned out to live in the town dump during Ulysses' absence, instantly knows him. Argos had no strength to go to him, but he lifted his head and wagged his tail, meeting Ulysses' eyes with a gaze of longing and love. As Ulysses' eyes flooded with tears, the old dog died. Ulysses sees that nonhuman recognition and loyalty and realizes that it's enough. He returns to his journeys knowing that he has been seen and accepted by the universe through the eyes of the faithful Argos.

Faccia Bello's life span had been extended to provide a source of compassion and unconditional love for me, which I now was learning to mirror. I felt a deepening gratitude for the personal interest the natural world was extending toward my soul.

The Shaman Bulldog

I was sensing the presence and the expression of the divine within Faccia Bello. He was a walking, snoring, barking manifestation of the source of life, for which I was very grateful.

8

A Little Death

*Every spiritual tradition advises the same:
Keep the thought of death near. Don't run
from it. . . . The ego grows bloated by the
denial of death; the spirit grows strong and
gentle living in its presence.*

—SAM KEEN
Hymns to an Unknown God

As Faccia Bello grew in age and the wisdom of his native clan, I had begun to search for answers in the mystery of my own life. Alone with my bulldog, I found that writing became a way to meditate. Art and poetry were new adventures, new ways of looking at my world. I was soon to discover how art can seize us when we least expect it, revealing things unknown to our conscious minds.

In an intuitive flash, I began writing about Faccia Bello one day. Without conscious effort, the details of his "little death" poured from my pen as images of labored breathing and gradual weight loss flashed in my mind.

I began to write his obituary before the fact, a prophetic preparation for the loss I would feel at his passing. I hoped I was writing fiction, but the words had an awful ring of truth.

Very soon I saw words and imagination collide with reality, as Faccia Bello appeared to enter another decline in health.

Following the radical face lift to clear his irritated eyes, Faccia Bello's face had taken on the heartbreaking countenance of a tragic clown. His eyes had some tenacious mucus every morning, especially the left eye, which remained chronically infected. Twice a day it required washing with iso-tears and antibiotic ointment.

So it came to be a daily ritual of which he had grown tired. "Medication time" was now fraught with gamesmanship and struggle. When he sensed he was being approached with the cleaning materials, he would duck under the coffee table or fly out through a doggie door and duck into his kennel cave, gaining a brief postponement.

I began to notice how much food was left unfinished after his morning and evening feeding. Faccia was a good eater and in his prime years weighed eighty-two pounds. As he aged, switching him to senior food slimmed him down until he carried seventy pounds with great dignity and more mobility. He relished large beef-flavored bone biscuits and little supplements of tuna or scrambled eggs mixed with his normal food. A little pasta and clams were treats as well. He wouldn't work for extra-small treats but won them nevertheless by his mournful, pleading looks. Now Faccia Bello often ignored his food.

By October he had lost fourteen pounds. His huge muscular chest and solid shoulder muscle were diminished to a thin coat, sinew, and bone. His spine and ribs were visible, and he began occasionally to vomit up his food. No combination of food or gruel stayed down. I would have to take him to the animal hospital, weigh him, and leave him for a workup.

How much Faccia Bello suffered, he couldn't say. Much of his behavior was still normal. For animals we have no comfort-making drugs. Pain persists until someone ends it. Death by starvation is one of the grimmer ways to transcend this life. He was now fifty-six pounds.

I had him admitted to the animal hospital for a full workup, which took two to three days and included an upper GI, small bowel and colon x-rays, labwork, gastroscopy, and even a small bowel biopsy. As always, I waited helplessly. I was worn out from trying to care for him.

I recalled what the poets and ancient writers believed. There is a timeless purpose and a rhythm moving our souls through ordinary time. It's the hard times, the times of loss, that crack the husk of love's seeds wide open.

The modern machine world says we have the technology to fix the bad times, if not now, then in the near future. As a radiologist I work daily with the technology, trying to find cures for human frailty.

I believe the poets rather than the technicians.

Grace has manifested all along the way as well, or I would have surely been overcome. In this present moment as I write about past events, I'm aware of how much support and comfort I have received, always there in every moment, just beyond awareness. I try to practice a rhythmic stopping many times during the day to allow meditation and centering, to open to the infusion of our Ally's support and comfort.

As I waited for Faccia Bello, I began thanking God for sustenance and yielded to a moment of trust that Faccia Bello and I would both be supported by this flowing grace, whatever the outcome. Faccia Bello was facing another of his life-threatening waves, and I was on the verge of surrendering, of seeing his death as an end to suffering.

Faccia Bello's x-rays showed the stomach wasn't obstructed by a tumor mass, but it wouldn't empty. Large, distended, without life or tone for contraction, it was now just a nonfunctioning sack. The rest of the bowel was similar, dilated with a loss of surface folds and markings. This was the pattern of inflammatory bowel disease.

Faccia Bello had been on long-term antibiotic therapy for his chronic eye and sinus infections, and like humans, he had eventually acquired a membranous gastritis and inflammatory bowel. The medicine with which we had tried to cure him had now brought him to the edge of death.

Faccia Bello's internist prescribed acid-blocking agents, prednisone, bowel motility medication, and a high-density diet, plus a different antibiotic for the infections. Faccia would eventually come home to more intensive care.

The Shaman Bulldog

While I was waiting in the treatment room at the animal hospital, my imagination took flight and I began to see images fired as if from a dream. I realized that this was a mystical and magical place of urban shaman healers, all serving the animal nation. People were bustling around in forest green clothes, bending over frightened sick animals.

Consciously or not, they were following ancient traditions of healing. They were applying their art to members of that nonverbal "other nation" who needed our medical expertise as much as we needed their love and companionship.

I also began to see myself in a new light. As a medical healer, I am a practitioner of that ancient energy and magic, using modern technology to practice original medicine.

Watching the vets at the hospital, I began to realize in a direct mainline shot of magic that the ordinary sights of our lives are really quite extraordinary. Henry Beston learned this same thing by living in a cottage on Cape Cod for a year, just watching the local and migratory birds.

Every Christmas I had sent these wonderful animal healers a box of chocolates and signed the card "Faccia Bello." The attention and fuss they made over him was amazing. They kept him at the hospital two weeks, adjusting the medication and gradually bringing him back to eating normally. Faccia Bello was on the mend again, enjoying fine dining and getting fat.

So he came home eating and picking up weight, back over sixty pounds and on the way up to sixty-six pounds. He preferred not only the standard meals, but the in-between-meal snacks that sick folks can have.

I watched him sleep spread-eagle on the cool Mexican tile floor. Breathing is a great task for him, very bubbly and noisy. A massive energy and life force pulls down his diaphragm and expands the large chest, air entering reluctantly through his narrow nasal channels and sinuses.

Each breath is fascinating. It is a natural work of art on display, synchronous animal power pulling life into the body one sweeping breath at a time, an earth creature signaling without alarm the hope of life. My breath is quiet and shallow, and in that silence I fail to discern the underlying dramatic presence of life.

Faccia Bello's deep snores reverberate through the room as he sleeps, his beefy red tongue resting on the floor, with its moisture connected to the earth. The guy can snore. It has been such comforting music, dramatic and operatic, flowing throughout the home for so many years, keeping time with events of our lives.

His resting and sleeping makes music of each breath. I whisper his name. One eye opens. Is he on the bridge between two worlds?

He had faced a little death as we all do, an inch at a time. These episodes always help to bring about for me a growing sense of my own mortality. A little death is always dancing behind the veils of life, and recognizing this makes each day sweet in its own way.

Faccia Bello will have no obituary yet. His "little death" is part of his living testimony.

9

All Has Been Prepared

And because I had known this outer and
secret world, and been able to live as I had
lived, reverence and gratitude greater and
deeper than ever possessed me, sweeping every
emotion else aside, and space and silence an
instant closed together over life.

—HENRY BESTON

Although Faccia Bello gained weight, by
December his chronic sinus infection was
not responding to the new antibiotic. Tomaso
tried to clean it out, but the tissue was necrotic
and bleeding. Decaying material was spreading

the infection, and his breathing became much more difficult.

Tomaso gave me more medications, but Faccia Bello refused to eat, even the tasty little treats that I used to wrap up his medicines and try to smuggle them into his mouth. He ignored his food dish.

He did respond to the feminine influence that had entered both our lives. A dream had revealed to me that a woman acquaintance would soon become both lover and soulmate. She is a lover of animals, and as she and I grew closer, she fell in love with Faccia Bello as well. When he quit eating, she looked deep into his eyes, saw the suffering and pain there, and told me that he had decided to die. I felt that he knew I was no longer alone and could leave without regret.

Knowing that he was slipping away and powerless to stop his suffering, I called Tomaso to make the final arrangement for the next morning. Medical care and loving had no more to offer, and his misery now was clearly needless. Faccia Bello was bound to my heart strings, and the pain I was feeling was both his and mine. Over time, through trials, love, and suffering, we had achieved unity.

All Has Been Prepared

♦

Faccia Bello laid his head on the cool tile floor. There was no longer any hunger. He shuddered with the energy of his labored breathing.

He slipped in and out of the Dreamtime easily now. Sister Death was very close, sighing at his shoulder and whispering to him out of the shadows. He closed his eyes, his head drooping. Maybe this time he could go into the Dreamtime and not have to come back.

As Faccia Bello settled into darkness, ancient images emerged and shifted shape in his dream. Through oceanic expanses of time, his soul drifted. He floated lazily above sunlit, timeless plains, vast drifts of sand and mud, icy plateaus and craggy monoliths with their sturdy and unyielding presence. Sinking into the fog-shrouded depths of time, he saw the ancestors of his feathered friends, leather-winged reptiles who had terrorized the land, and he saw finned creatures struggling toward the sunlight, crawling out of the ocean depths to take their first gasping breaths.

In a dark starlit night, he found the old Woman again, sitting by the campfire with the yellow-eyed Wolf. She told him again the stories of creation, and the night so long ago when Man and Dog first became friends.

"As the Man sat by a campfire, hugging its warmth, a loping shape emerged from the darkness. The Wolf's stomach grumbled hungrily as he stared at the Man's food roasting on the fire. Yellow eyes met brown eyes. In his loneliness, the Man tore off a chunk of meat and laid it on the ground, an offering to this shaggy, fierce creature. That night, eating together at the campfire, Man and Wolf pledged their eternal friendship and assistance. As Wolf's descendants, the Canines have kept their end of the bargain, but Man's pact regrettably has not been quite so loyally sustained."

The old Woman stood and motioned for Faccia Bello to follow her. He accompanied her into a large room bathed in light. There were many dogs there, all different shapes and sizes, magnificent creations with new bodies, shining coats, and a primitive intelligence gleaming in their dark eyes.

It was an ancient bestiary of spectral shapes and forms that had prowled through Man's unconscious since the beginning of time. Faccia Bello saw werewolves, half man and half wolf, and the loup-garou that stalks the New Orleans swamps. He saw a three-headed hound who guards the entrance to the Greek underworld, the four-eyed Persian dogs who conduct the dead across the Gate of Decision, and the Asian Dog of Many Colors who created the world. He saw ghosts dogs that roam the moors and whisper to men at night in their dreams, and the water dogs of Ireland that guard ocean treasures.

The old Woman told him that he was part of this magnificent array of creatures that dwelled deep in Man's unconscious. The Dog had long ago agreed to be a companion and helpmate to Man and did so now even in dreams. Some of these forms may even exist one day, she told Faccia Bello with a chuckle.

"Creation is still brewing. We have many surprising experiments in progress."

♦

My last night with Faccia Bello, I lit some candles and thanked God for the great gift of this companion. I then released him back to his clan and to the Earth Mother and the world of soul. I asked for his peace through the night. I welcomed Sister Death, and Faccia Bello rested easy on his couch as I read from Kahlil Gibran's *The Prophet,* "Joy and Sorrow." Tomaso would be waiting at 9:00 A.M. the next day to put him to sleep.

On the last morning I drummed on my African *djembe* and burned sage. I was the Death Band and the Mercy Band both, much like a New Orleans funeral. Finally I called his favorite phrase, "Faccia

Bello—bye-bye car!" It was the first time in many months that I had seen his puppylike enthusiasm for a new adventure. He bounced a few steps, his hindquarters waggling, then stood shakily at my feet. He needed to be lifted into the car.

As he rode to the vet's on the front seat, hints of his old curiosity and energy winked out of his clouded eyes. How could I let him go? What would life be like without him? I listened to his labored breathing and saw the pain in his glazed eyes. He had begun vomiting bile that morning.

My questions were overruled by the need for mercy. I couldn't stand to see him hurting any longer. I knew that Tomaso would do the right thing.

I carried Faccia Bello into the vet's office, back on the metal examining table, talking to him softly and brushing him. Tomaso checked him one last time and sighed. "He is ready to go," he said.

I whispered my last good-byes, and he was euthanized with a large dose of sodium pentothal. Peace at last, no more tortured breathing and pain. He collapsed easily into his familiar Sphinx posture, and his great head settled slowly on his forepaws as his large tongue turned purple blue. This time there would be no artificial respiration.

His suffering was over, and he had finished the great race.

I asked for cremation and an urn to keep his ashes. Tomaso told me there would be no final bill—Faccia Bello left the earth with his account paid in full. As I left for my office, an old jukebox song drifted into memory. *"And when one of us is gone, and one of us is left to carry on . . ."* Tears began to flow.

Remembering our life together, I saw in my imagination Faccia Bello's breakthrough to the next world and heard a small voice from within.

◆

"It's been a wonderful journey. We were magic together, for we saw each other with ancient eyes. Now I'm free of my body but always with you in your heart.

"Use my love to care for yourself. You are in me and I am in you and we made it sweet fun for each other."

◆

It was as if the universe spoke and assured me that I should celebrate this life so zestfully lived. A piece of Kahlil Gibran floated into consciousness: "The deeper that sorrow carves into your being, the more joy you can contain."

Many times since Faccia's death I've gone up and sat on our desert hill, both in early morning and twilight. I talk with the tall sentinel Saguaro cactus through my imaginal soul.

"I miss my boy. Have you any word of him?"

"Yes, he's back with his great animal nation, and his stories are quite wonderful. He remembers and lives on in your imagination and love. He's now part of a new consciousness of the Creator, fully alive and splendid."

All our work together hasn't been about smart, intellectual, or scholarly tasks. It's been about life and love, grief and pain, joy and magic. So what timing to end this here, with Faccia Bello lingering on in image and voice. Last night I was certain I heard him go outside and drink from the auto-faucet.

Now I can talk to cactus or a sparrow or desert mountain and hear their spirit in reply. Because I have been seen and loved by Faccia Bello, I know there are others out there, waiting in each ordinary moment. I see the power of the natural world waiting to touch my heart and inform my life.

Faccia Bello became my shaman's bag of magic tricks. My overused rational brain was silent a while, and a magical new world of the heart appeared, a world where transformation was natural.

Acknowledgments

Faccia Bello was a real bulldog, and we have chronicled some of his adventures and misadventures. I was fortunate to be Faccia Bello's companion and caretaker. The magic of the story is real, manifesting spontaneously as our two worlds merged. Faccia Bello's vet, Dr. Gabor Vajda, is a bulldog expert who supplied the miracle of love and healing many times to my crisis-prone companion. Some characters in the story are mythical or fictionalized, and the timeline has been altered to compress the story. Much of the folklore and myths regarding dogs is contained in Maria Leach's marvelous and comprehensive book *God Had a Dog*.

Faccia Bello had a magical effect on the people

who looked deeply in his eyes and beheld the soul. After death, he continued to weave his spell on those who made this book possible.

My most heartfelt thanks goes to my loving friend Ruth Cox, mentor at the Institute of Transpersonal Psychology in Palo Alto, California, who listened to countless bulldog tales. She has added invaluable insight, counsel, and awareness to my writing over the years.

"Renaldo, you must write the story of Faccia Bello. It will make you famous." I laughed when my friend Irene Grier, Ph.D., a psychologist and a counselor, made that remark. The friendship and intuitive support of this wise woman sparked the telling of this story. When we talk about Mr. Bello, tears well and words stop.

Henry Beston's poetic prose and perceptive observations of wildlife led him, and now me, to apprehend a desperate need to engage creation through mystical relationship. Shamanic, mystic, Sufi, and native traditions support his view. In one year of living on Cape Cod, Beston rediscovered the fathomless magic that is an everyday event in the world of nature. Quotations from him in this book are contained in *The Outermost House,* a most valuable resource for those investigating the natural realm.

ACKNOWLEDGMENTS

Beston was introduced to me by Michele St. George, a talented writer and editor who possesses a mystical connection to the natural world. At the end of Faccia Bello's life she cared for him and gave me the support I needed to stay in the moment and give the details of Faccia Bello's death the ending, grace, and dignity it deserved. I see this as further evidence of the graceful mystery inherent in bringing this story into being.

In another synchronous event, Michele was searching for a publisher for this manuscript when a book fell open to the name of Julie Castiglia's Literary Agency in California. Julie devoured Faccia Bello's story in a single sitting, her own dog by her side, and called to say she knew she could find it a home. Her talent, awareness, and knowledge of the publishing industry were another essential link in the chain of events. She warned us that we must find the right editor to give the book the care and attention it deserved.

Rob McQuilkin, our editor at Warner Books, became another protector of Faccia Bello's when he administered his own perception and talent to the story. Rob understands magic, and his invaluable criticism and incisive observations smoothed out the manuscript and made it as nearly perfect as it can be.